I'M AS HAPPY AS A...

DEBI K STINSON

First Printing, 2024

ISBN 979-8-9892641-6-2

To Katydid,
my first born,
my last born,
my heart.

An Ant with
an Apple

A Beaver with a Banana

A Cow with a Cookie

A Donkey with a Donut

An Egret with an Egg

A Frog with a French fry

A Goat with a Grilled cheese

A Hedgehog with a Hot dog

An Iguana with an Ice cream

A Jaguar with Jellybeans

A Kangaroo with a Kiwi

A Lamb with Lemonade

A Monkey with a Mango

A Narwhal with Nachos

An Octopus with Oatmeal

A Panda with a Pizza

A Quail with a Quiche

A Raccoon with a Radish

A Sloth with a Salad

A Turtle with a Taco

A Unicorn with an Upside-down cake

A **V**ulture with a **V**indaloo

A Walrus with a Waffle

A Xolo with
(show low)
a Xôi
(z-oy)

A Yak with
a Yam

A Zebra with a Zucchini

...Whenever
I'm with you

READING COMPREHENSION QUESTIONS

1. What food is paired with the Ant?
2. Find the animal that has a donut. What letter does it start with?
3. Which food matches with the Lamb?
4. How many animals are paired with a dessert?
5. What is the last animal and food pairing in the book?

LET'S CONNECT!
→
SCAN HERE

ABOUT THE AUTHOR

Debi K Stinson was born and raised in Royal, Alabama. She is a graduate of the University of Alabama and currently resides in Clarksville, Tennessee. She enjoys spending time with her family and working on her farm, Little Legacy. Her passion has always been children, animal rescues, and giving back to her community.